To Laura P. and Emily-Rose S.

IS IT CHRISTMAS?
A RED FOX BOOK 978 1 782 95587 0

First published in Great Britain by The Bodley Head,
an imprint of Random House Children's Publishers UK

The Bodley Head edition published 2003
Red Fox edition published 2004

3 5 7 9 10 8 6 4

Red Fox Books are published by Random House Children's Publishers UK
61–63 Uxbridge Road, London W5 5SA,
a division of The Random House Group Ltd,
in Australia by Random House Australia (Pty) Ltd,
20 Alfred Street, Milsons Point, Sydney, NSW 2061, Australia,
in New Zealand by Random House New Zealand Ltd,
18 Poland Road, Glenfield, Auckland 10, New Zealand,
and in South Africa by Random House (Pty) Ltd,
Endulini, 5A Jubilee Road, Parktown 2193, South Africa

THE RANDOM HOUSE GROUP Limited Reg. No. 954009
www.**randomhousechildrens**.co.uk

A CIP catalogue record for this book is available from the British Library.

Printed in China

Is It Christmas?

JOHN PRATER

RED FOX

"Is it Christmas?" asked Baby Bear, early one morning.
"No, not yet," said Grandbear, "but after two more
sleeps, it will be."
Baby Bear finished breakfast and bounced
downstairs to help Grandbear.

On the mat were lots of cards.
They opened them up
and hung them on ribbons.

Then Baby Bear made lovely cards to send
to all their family and friends.

They scrubbed
and polished the
whole house.

Baby Bear was
a big help!

Then they baked lots
of biscuits and cakes.
"Why are we
making so
many?" asked
Baby Bear.

"They're for our special Christmas
visitors," said Grandbear.

What a busy day! Soon,
it was bedtime again.

"Is it Christmas?" asked Baby Bear, early the next morning. "Are our visitors here?"
"Soon," said Grandbear, "after one more sleep it will be Christmas, and they'll be here."

"We're going
to bring in
the tree today,"
said Grandbear.
"A tree? Inside
the house?"
laughed Baby Bear.
"Of course," said Grandbear, "our Christmas tree."
But when they opened the door,
they both gasped.

"It's all white!" shouted Baby Bear.
"I thought it might snow," said Grandbear.

"Wow!" said Baby Bear,
running outside,

making big footprints
in the snow,

and catching
snowflakes.

Grandbear joined in the fun.

They threw snowballs at each other.
Grandbear seemed to miss every time . . .

. . . but Baby Bear didn't.

Then they rolled some very big snowballs and made a jolly snowbear.

Baby Bear got a
lift to the top of
the hill,

and a ride all the way down. Wheeeeee!

"Now then, let's find our Christmas tree," said Grandbear.

"This one?" asked
Baby Bear.
"That's far too big,"
said Grandbear.

"This one?" asked
Baby Bear.
"That's much too small,"
said Grandbear.

"... But this one is just right."

Grandbear dug it up, and carried it home,
wondering why it felt so heavy.

Grandbear dragged the tree indoors.

Baby Bear helped
to plant it in
a great big pot.

"Do we climb up it now?" asked Baby Bear.
"No, we do something that's better
than that," said Grandbear.

"We decorate it."

They
decorated
the tree from
top to bottom,
and then
the rest of
the room.
"Wow!" said
Baby Bear.

"There's just one more
thing . . ." said Grandbear.

". . . the lights!"
"Oooh," said Baby Bear, "they're like twinkly stars!"

It all looked so wonderful, that Baby Bear didn't
want to come to the table for dinner. So they sat
by the tree and had a cosy picnic.

"It's Christmas tomorrow," said Grandbear,
"and our special visitors will be here."

"That's nice," yawned Baby Bear, sleepily.

"Just one more sleep," whispered Grandbear.

Later that night, while Baby Bear slept, someone left some presents under the Christmas tree.

"Is it Christmas?"
asked Baby Bear,
early the next
morning.
"Yes it is!" said
Grandbear.

"YIPPEE!"
shouted
Baby Bear.

There was a loud knock at the front door.
"Listen, they're here!" said Grandbear.
"Who?" asked Baby Bear.
"Our special visitors," said Grandbear.
"Who?" asked
Baby Bear again.

"The whole family," said Grandbear.
"Happy Christmas, Baby Bear!" they shouted.
"Happy Christmas, everyone!" said Baby Bear.

Other Baby Bear books to share:

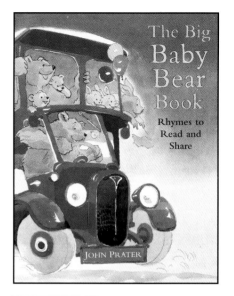

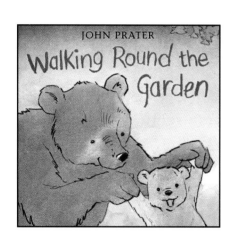

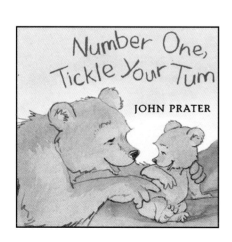

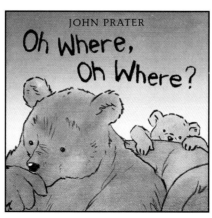